UNTIL
WE WIN

UNTIL WE WIN

Linda Newbery

Barrington Stoke

First published in 2017 in Great Britain by
Barrington Stoke Ltd
18 Walker Street, Edinburgh, EH3 7LP

www.barringtonstoke.co.uk

Text © 2017 Linda Newbery

A CIP catalogue record for this book is available
from the British Library upon request

ISBN: 978-1-78112-579-3

Printed in China by Leo

Contents

*For Jane Sandell, inspirational librarian,
with thanks for friendship and support over
many years*

Summer, 1914. I'll never forget it.

No one else will, either, because the war with Germany started in August.

But for me, it was the year I became a suffragette. The year I found something to fight for and someone to spend my life with. And it was the year I went to prison.

It seems ridiculous now, doesn't it, that only men could vote back then? And that women had such a long struggle to win the same right? But that's how it was.

I was 17 that year, and the battle for Votes for Women had been going on for as long as I could remember. It was always in the papers – suffragettes who had smashed windows, tried

to get into Buckingham Palace, even set fire to post-boxes.

None of that had much to do with life in our village.

Everything changed for me when I bought my bicycle. I'd saved from my wages since I started work, and at last I could afford one. It wasn't smart or even new, but second-hand. Its paint was chipped here and there and its wicker basket was a bit shabby. But it was *mine* – my pride and joy. With a bicycle of my own I could go wherever I wanted – as soon as I learned to ride it.

CHAPTER 1

Freedom

When I heard hoof-beats behind me, I knew I was in for a teasing.

The riders – my brother Ted and his friend, Frank – were exercising the hunt horses. Both boys were two years older than me, and they thought themselves grand and important, perched up high in their saddles. I'd have thought myself grand too, if I could ride one of those lovely horses. Ted always rode dappled-grey Sea Spray, while Frank had the master's horse, Blackbird. Each of them held a second

horse on a leading-rein, so the lane was full of clatter and snorting and head-tossing.

I wished they hadn't come along *now*! I'd never sat on a bicycle before and it was trickier than I thought. As soon as I hoicked myself up to the saddle and found the second pedal with my foot, the front wheel wobbled into the grass bank, and I tipped over.

That's where I was, picking myself up, when the horses drew level. Sea Spray snorted and pranced. I tried to turn round while I was half-on and half-off my bicycle, gripping the handlebars as hard as I could.

"You'll never ride that thing," Frank called out, laughing. "You want four legs, not two wheels."

"I will!" I panted. "Wait and see."

Frank was Ted's best friend, but I didn't much like him. I didn't like the hunt, either –

what fun could there be in chasing a poor fox to death?

But our family depended on the Valley Foxhounds. Ted worked for them, and my father was a blacksmith – he shod the hunt horses, as well as every other horse and pony in the village. The yard next to our cottage was always full of the smell of smoke and burning hoof, the ring of hammer on iron and the scrape of new shoes on cobbles. There was no hunting now, in July, but cub-hunting would begin in August, as soon as the harvest was in.

"Your skirt's caught up," Frank said, as I struggled with my bicycle. "You want some of those pantaloons!"

He was right. My skirt *was* in the way, and it had tangled itself round my legs. But I hadn't got any pantaloons – bloomers, most people called them – and I wasn't likely to get any. Only fashionable ladies in towns wore bloomers for bicycling. Some of them got jeered at for

looking 'blooming ridiculous', but they weren't the sort of women to care about that.

I steadied my bike and pushed it into a gateway.

"We'll pull you out of the ditch on our way back," Ted told me and Frank laughed, not in a nice way. It sounded as if he'd really like to see me fall off.

When they were past, I gritted my teeth for another try. If I fell over again, at least no one would see.

This time I did better. With my bottom firmly on the leather saddle and a foot on each pedal I wobbled for a few yards and almost crashed, but then I pushed on and found that I could balance. As I pressed down on the pedals and gained speed, the wind tugged my hat right off my head, but I didn't stop to pick it up. The road stretched ahead.

This was what I'd saved up for.

No more waiting for the bus to town, or rushing for the last one back to the village. I was the proud owner of a bicycle. Now I could go wherever I wanted.

Freedom – wonderful freedom!

CHAPTER 2

In the Coffee House

I practised riding my bike on Sunday afternoon. Soon I felt more confident and could bowl along with hardly a wobble. After church, dinner and the washing-up, there were a few spare hours before I had to help get the tea.

Ted never helped in the kitchen. When he came home from the stables he sprawled in a chair or sat at the table and expected Mother and me to wait on him. I blamed her for that.

"He's a working man, your brother," she would say. "He deserves his rest."

Ted had started off as a groom, but last winter the master Mr Colson promoted him to whipper-in. This meant that on hunting days he rode out with the hounds, all dressed up in a red jacket and polished boots, on lovely Sea Spray.

I worked, too, but that didn't seem to matter. I still helped my mother to cook the meals and do the washing and the cleaning. It was never-ending – scrubbing floors and brushing carpets that would soon get dirty again, and struggling to hang heavy sheets on the washing line.

"It's good training for when you get married, and have your own family to look after," Mother would say, as she rubbed her red, sore hands.

I hated that thought, especially when I saw Ted smirking. Even worse, he had a way of giving orders, and that made me mad.

9

"Another cup of tea, Lizzy!" he would say – no *please*, as if I were a servant. Or, "Where's my shirt, Lizzy? Haven't you ironed it yet?"

Sometimes I'd snap back, "Do it yourself!" But Mother would say, "Now, now, Lizzy. Ironing's not a man's job."

I was glad of my job at Palmer and Dawes Insurance Office – it got me away from the chores at home – but, to tell the truth, I was already a bit bored with it. It paid my weekly wages and it took me to the busy town of Denham, six miles away. Our village was full of itself and its gossip, but there was a bigger world beyond. I wanted to be part of that.

I'd started work at Palmer and Dawes last summer, when I was 16. My parents were proud of me. They said it was a cut above being a maid or a factory girl. Or taking in washing and ironing, which was how Mother earned money for the family.

"You were always good at your lessons," Father said, "even if you were cheeky with it."

It was odd how school seemed different to me now. All the years I was there, I hadn't seen the point of my lessons. I wanted to be outside with my friends, not sitting at a desk for hours. But now – if I were back there I'd learn everything I could, to make more of myself.

At the office I did the filing – putting folders and letters away in drawers and on dusty shelves. I fetched things for Mr Palmer and old Mr Dawes, and sorted out the post every morning and afternoon.

It was Mr Dawes, the senior partner, who told me that I ought to learn shorthand and typewriting. Then, he said, he could dictate letters to me for typing up later.

"Shorthand?" I asked. I'd never heard of it.

"It's a way of writing down words really fast, using lines and dashes," he explained.

"Watch this." He made some squiggles on a bit of paper and showed me. "That says *writing down words really fast*," he told me. "See, I wrote the marks just as fast as I could say the words. If you learned shorthand and typewriting you could do a lot more than filing. You'd earn more, too."

I liked Mr Dawes. He was kinder and less strict than Mr Palmer, his son-in-law. Once I overheard them talking about me.

"Please don't give Miss Frost ideas above her station," Mr Palmer was saying. They were walking down the front steps, and they didn't see me behind them with a bundle of letters for the post office. "She's only an office junior. With a great deal to learn."

Mr Dawes answered, "Oh, but she's clever, that one. Bright as a button. And when the new girl starts we can give Miss Frost more to do."

Clever? No one had called me that before. I was more used to them calling me a fidget or a chatterbox.

But I was glad about the new girl. Perhaps we could be friends. Everyone else at Palmer and Dawes was twice my age at least.

Later, when Billy the errand-boy brought a parcel, Mr Palmer told me off. "I don't pay you to waste your time chatting and giggling, Miss Frost! Get back to your work."

"Yes, sir," I muttered, and I tried not to laugh as Billy made clown faces behind Mr Palmer's back.

Well, I never did learn shorthand. But it was thanks to Mr Dawes that I met Julia and Elsie, and joined the fight for Votes for Women.

He told me about a weekly evening class for shorthand that was starting in Waltham, at the Workers' Institute. Waltham was five miles from Denham where the office was. It was too

13

far to walk, and there was no bus back after five o'clock. But with my bicycle, I could get there!

The class was on Thursdays. By that first Thursday I was riding my bicycle to and from work. My parents and even Ted were getting used to this. Mother always stood by the front door to wave me off, and I think maybe she felt a little bit proud.

Waltham was a larger town than Denham, with a big Town Hall and a market twice a week, and there was a railway station with trains to London. I found the Workers' Institute in Fishmarket Street, and left my bicycle there. I had nearly an hour to spare before the class. I was thirsty after my ride, and it was a long while since my lunch of bread and cheese.

I saw a coffee house in the market square, and thought I'd go in for a cup of tea and maybe a cake. It was wonderful to feel like

a modern young woman who could cycle into town and go to a café alone.

I went to a corner table and a waitress took my order. There were only two other customers, a pair of well-dressed young women. They looked at me and smiled, and one of them asked, "Are you here for the meeting?"

"What meeting?" I didn't think she meant the shorthand class.

"The W.S.P.U. meeting. In the Mission Hall."

I noticed the badges they both wore on their jackets. Behind them, on a coat-stand, were two felt hats. Each had a band of ribbons of purple, green and white. So these two were suffragettes – campaigners for Votes for Women!

I knew about the suffragettes, of course. I'd read about them in the newspapers, and I knew that W.S.P.U. stood for Women's Social and Political Union. I was astonished by the

bravery of some of those women. One had died after running in front of the King's horse in the Derby. I remembered that Ted's sympathy was all for the horse. "Stupid woman got what she deserved, if you ask me!" he grumbled. "What was she thinking? That horse could have been killed!" Emily Wilding Davison, her name was. I remembered that because her funeral had been in the newspaper.

"Are you a supporter?" the young woman asked me. Her friend hadn't spoken yet, but she was watching me closely. She was a bit older – in her mid-twenties, maybe.

"Yes," I said. "I mean no." And then I felt bad because I hadn't done anything – just waited to see what would happen. "I mean, not *yet*," I explained. "Of course women must have the vote."

"Won't you come and join us?" the friend said, and she patted the spare seat at their table.

They were so friendly that I couldn't resist.
I moved across, and the waitress came over
with my scone and pot of tea. The older woman
asked my name and introduced herself as Julia,
Mrs Julia Harrold. Her friend was Elsie Roberts.

"Julia's our speaker for tonight," Elsie said.
"She'll be telling us about her time in prison,
and the Cat and Mouse Act."

"You've been in prison!" I said.

"Yes, Lizzy. Several times," Julia told me.
She had a way of looking at me very straight,
as if she'd like to read my thoughts.

"If you'd like to hear all about it," Elsie said,
"why don't you come to the meeting?"

CHAPTER 3

Cat and Mouse

"Well, Lizzy," Mr Dawes said, next morning. "How did you like the shorthand?"

"Oh –" I felt myself redden. "I didn't go to the class after all. I – wasn't well."

I didn't like lying to kind Mr Dawes, but I was going to have to tell more lies, since last night.

He said no more, because Connie, the new girl, was starting work and he wanted me to help her.

"You'll find Lizzy knows her way around," he told her, "so ask her if you're not sure about anything."

Connie looked a little younger than me, and was slender and pale, with neat dark hair pinned up into a bun. Her large blue eyes pleaded with me to be friendly. I was glad to help, because now she was the office junior, while I felt more important.

I showed her how to sort the letters into trays and helped her to read Mr Palmer's crabby handwriting. "I know," I told her, and smiled. "It's awful but you'll get used to it."

I had to force myself to concentrate. My mind was sparking with excitement and a new determination. Last night I had found something bigger than myself, bigger than the samey dullness of life in the village and the office. I'd found something to feel passionate about.

19

Passion was what Julia and Elsie and the other women felt – I saw it shining from them, bright and true. It was only right that women should vote and they – we! – wouldn't give up until that happened.

When Julia stood up, her voice was low but confident. Her words held everyone riveted. She told us about Holloway Prison, and how she had gone on hunger strike and refused food and drink for days. Then a doctor came to her cell, and burly prison warders held her down. While she struggled and fought, they pushed a tube up her nose and down her throat and poured gruel into her. Afterwards she was bruised and torn, bent over in pain. I felt myself wince as Julia described it, and I saw women in the rows in front of me sobbing and reaching for their hankies.

"This happened twice each day," she told us, "and several times I thought I would die."

She wasn't making a drama of it, but I knew it must have been agony.

"But the government won't defeat us," she said in her clear voice. "We will never give in. And now there will be no more force-feeding. If this carried on, someone *would* die, and that would look bad for them. That's why they've brought in the Cat and Mouse Act, as we call it. When a prisoner is weak from starvation, they let her go free – until she recovers and shows herself in public. Then they can arrest her again. It's like a cat playing with a mouse. Which just shows how the men of our government still think of us. Like mice. In spite of everything."

It was a warm and sunny day, so at dinner time I took Connie to the park. She hadn't brought

anything to eat, so we shared my bread and cheese.

I was still caught up in the excitement of last night, and I couldn't help telling Connie.

"It was so *stirring*! If you'd been there, you'd have thought so too. I'm going to join, properly join. There's a rally on Saturday, in Hyde Park, and I'm going. And to more meetings. You could come, too," I added, seeing that Connie was quiet.

Connie bit her lip. "All the way to London?"

"Why not?" I asked. "I shall go on the train. Come on! It'll be fun to go together."

Connie didn't look too sure. "They wouldn't like it at home."

"*My* family won't like it, either," I told her. "But that's the point. We're women." Up till last night I would have described Connie and me as *girls*. "We're strong," I went on. "We're

22

capable. If we let people tell us what to do, nothing will change."

I cycled home after work between fields of barley and ditches lush with meadowsweet. My spirits flew high as the skylarks as I rode, fast and confident now, along the lane.

Someone waved from the track that led to the hunt kennels. It was Frank, on his way home – there was no sign of Ted. I stopped to see what he wanted, and gave him a big smile. He grinned back in his cocky way, holding the stub of a cigarette between his fingers.

"I'll walk with you," he said.

"But I'm on my bike."

"Well, let me push it." He dropped the cigarette and ground it out with his boot. "Then we can talk."

"What about?"

I was curious enough to let him take the handlebars. I got down and tugged my skirt straight as we walked on side by side.

"People say there's going to be a war," Frank said.

"What if there is?" I'd heard the rumours about a war with Germany. But it was easy to dismiss them as nothing more than talk.

"I shall join the Army," he said. "Ted will, too."

I turned to him, puzzled. "Why are you telling me this?"

"Because when I go, I'd like to have a sweetheart at home." He looked at me. "You, I mean."

I burst out laughing.

"What's funny?" he said. "I mean it."

We'd reached the slope before the village where the lane passed through woods on both sides. Frank glanced round, then stopped walking and took my arm.

"I like you, Lizzy," he said. "And I know you like me, too."

Before I could protest, he leaned towards me, still gripping my arm. Next moment his mouth was on mine and his arm round me, squeezing. I tasted cigarette smoke on his breath. Then I spluttered and pulled free.

"Stop it!" I shouted. "What are you *doing?*"

He still held my bike with his other hand. I grabbed the handlebars from him and pushed it out into the lane.

"Don't be a tease, Lizzy!" He looked pleased with himself. "Don't pretend you didn't want me to kiss you."

Kiss? It hadn't felt like a kiss – more like being pushed about.

"I didn't, and I don't!" I fired back. "What's got into you?"

He'd gripped my arm so hard that I still felt the press of his fingers. And *tease?* I'd done nothing to make him think I wanted it. My hands trembled and my heart pounded as I mounted my bicycle and rode away as fast as I could go.

At home, I wheeled my bicycle into the shed as usual, then stomped into the kitchen.

"What's the matter?" my mother asked, and Ted gave me a curious look from his seat at the table.

I was stirred up. Before I had met Frank, I'd been alight with excitement and happiness. Now I felt anger and confusion. Even a burn of shame, though I wasn't sure why.

"Frank says there'll be a war," I said, for something to say.

"Oh, you've been talking to Frank, have you?" Mother was filling the kettle. "Such a nice young man. And sweet on you, I've noticed."

Ted gave me a smirky look.

"Well," I snapped, "I'm not sweet on *him*."

"That can soon change," my mother said. "You could do a lot worse. It might settle you down a bit, if you had a sweetheart."

I couldn't stay in the room – I was too furious with Frank and now with both of them. I went straight upstairs and flung my hat down on the bed.

CHAPTER 4

Purple, White and Green

On Saturday I had to tell another lie. Well, a sort of lie. I said that I was going to Waltham after work finished at noon, and I let my mother think it was for a shopping trip.

"You young girls," she said with a sigh. "As soon as you earn money, it trickles through your fingers. What are you after? A new hat? Hair ribbons?"

Any ribbons I bought would be purple, white and green! I knew she thought I wanted something pretty to impress Frank, in spite of

what I'd said. It would be useful to let her think
that, for times like this when I wanted to slip
away without explaining where.

Today I was heading for the railway station,
not the shops. Elsie and I had arranged to meet
there and catch the train together. When we
got to Hyde Park, we'd try to find Julia – she
was already in London, staying with a friend.

We got on a bus at Liverpool Street Station
and sat on the top deck, which was open to the
sky. It was exciting to look out at the busy
streets, the tall buildings, the throngs of people
and buses and horses. I didn't tell Elsie that I'd
never been to London before. I'd seen pictures,
and now I was looking at it all for myself,
trying to take in everything I saw.

When we got off at Hyde Park Corner there
was a huge crowd – almost all women. Some
held banners and placards, and most wore
sashes, hats and rosettes in the suffragette
colours – purple, white and green. Just as I

was wishing I had something special to wear too, Elsie took two sashes out of her bag, and handed one to me. She worked for a dressmaker in town, and she had sewn them in secret.

With my sash on, I felt as proud as a soldier in uniform. Now I really felt part of this.

"We'll never find Julia," Elsie said, as we pushed our way through the throng.

A woman stood on a box in front of the crowd. She had a megaphone, but still I had to strain my ears.

"How is it that a man is allowed to vote, when no woman can?" she demanded. "Even if he's a drunkard, a bully, a layabout? A woman can be clever, responsible, well-informed – but she has no say. To be female is to be second-class. That has to change, and change now. The laws of this country were made by men. We will carry on breaking those laws until we

have the vote. Until women play their part in *making* the laws."

There was clapping as she stepped down, then a swell of excitement. Another woman, small and neat, stepped up to the box.

Elsie grabbed my arm. "It's Mrs Pankhurst! They said she might come!"

I stared and stared. This was Mrs Pankhurst herself – Emmeline Pankhurst, our great suffragette leader. She was elegant in her bonnet and gloves, but despite her smartness, she looked thin, even ill.

"She's just out of prison," Elsie whispered. "Now she'll be arrested and taken back."

This was how the Cat and Mouse Act worked, I remembered.

Still, I was happy to see the great lady for myself! Never before had I seen anyone famous.

There was *shhhh*ing all around, and voices fell silent as Mrs Pankhurst began to speak.

"Thank you all for supporting this glorious cause." Her voice was clear and sure. "The government must learn that we will never give in. Never, while there is breath in our bodies. Never, until we win."

I wanted to capture every word, to keep in my memory for always. Her words had lit up something inside me. I wasn't just watching from a distance. I was part of a team – an army, even. I felt that I'd be glad to go to prison, to be part of something so brave, so glorious.

Not everyone agreed. Someone yelled, "Shame!" and an egg flew through the air. It missed Mrs Pankhurst but it spattered on the coat of a policeman near by.

There was a ripple of laughter, and a scuffle broke out near the man who had thrown the egg. Then I heard shouts of "Deeds not words!"

This gave the police a reason to break up the meeting. Dozens of them ran in among us, with their wooden truncheons raised. The crowd surged. I saw some women hurry away while others stood their ground, defiant. Mrs Pankhurst was surrounded, but a group of women around her kicked and hit the policemen as they closed in. Mrs Pankhurst did not struggle, and two officers led her away, each holding her by the arm. Her dignity and stillness made them look foolish.

"She expected this," Elsie told me.

"Bullies!" a woman's voice yelled. "Beat and badger us all you like. Manhandle us and take us to prison. We'll never give in!"

"Never give in!" I found myself shouting with the others. My voice was loud and strong as I joined in the battle-cry.

Another woman climbed up on the box to speak. We listened for a while, but the main event was over. Mrs Pankhurst was gone and we never did find Julia.

On the train home, Elsie leaned towards me. "So, are you really with us?" she asked. "Committed?"

"Yes, of course!"

"Good. Then I'll see you in the coffee house on Thursday, same time as before."

When we parted, and I took off my sash to give it back, Elsie told me that it was mine to keep. I was thrilled. At home in my bedroom I folded it carefully and hid it in a drawer. I couldn't wait to wear it again, at the meeting on Thursday. I was a real suffragette now.

CHAPTER 5

A Pair of Silly Girls

There was a kind of sadness about Connie. At first I thought it was because she was anxious about her work, but after a few days I wondered if she was unhappy at home. Her blue eyes were often shiny, as if tears were waiting to be spilled. She didn't smile often, but smiling made her beautiful. I don't think she knew that.

Connie lived near Denham with her parents – there were no brothers or sisters. When I asked whether she had as many chores at home as I did, she only said, "There's always

a lot to do." For a moment she seemed about to say more, then she cast her eyes down and went back to her files.

I was curious, but after the London rally my head was full of a new idea, and I could think of little else.

At dinner-break on Monday we went to the park again, and sat in the shade of a big chestnut tree. I just had to tell her – it was a kind of boasting, I suppose. I wanted Connie to like me. And I wanted to make her smile.

"Can you keep a secret?" I asked.

"Of course I can!"

No one was near, but still I leaned close. "I'm going to get up very early tomorrow and carve VOTES FOR WOMEN on the golf course, on one of the greens," I told her. "Cut big letters into the grass."

Connie stared. "You won't!"

"I will."

Elsie had told me that other suffragettes had done this, on courses where Members of Parliament played golf. I didn't know if any MPs played at Waltham Links, but still I would make my point. I wanted to impress Elsie and Julia when I met them on Thursday. I wanted to prove my worth.

"What if you get into trouble?" Connie whispered.

"Probably no one will see me," I said. "If they do, I can run fast." Then it occurred to me. "Do you want to come too?"

"I couldn't!" Connie put a hand to her mouth.

"If there's any trouble, I'll take the blame," I told her.

She looked at me. "Yes, then. Yes, Lizzy, I'll do it. You're my friend now."

I felt myself glowing with excitement.
For the rest of the day, whenever I looked at
Connie, I couldn't help smiling, and sometimes
she gave me a small secret smile in return.

Soon I had everything planned. I'd bring
two sharp knives from my father's toolbox, the
ones he used for trimming horses' hooves. And
I'd already collected a bag of coal dust from our
bunker. I'd sneak out and meet Connie at the
golf course at half-past four in the morning,
soon after first light. Then we'd do the job and
go back to our homes for breakfast as usual.
Easy. No one need know where we'd been.

We were both worried about waking up in
time, but I left my curtains open so that the
first light of dawn roused me from sleep. I
dressed as fast as I could and crept out into the
windy grey morning.

When I reached the golf course I stood
looking at the final hole, by the club-house. I'd
decided to mark out the words first, in coal

dust – VOTES FOR WOMEN. Then we'd cut out the letters with our knives.

The grass was as smooth as green velvet. It was a pity to spoil it, but that was the plan. I had imagined big, neat letters, but sometimes the black dust spilled out in a rush, and sometimes it blew away on the wind. I was finishing a clumsy O when Connie arrived.

We started to cut, and that turned out to be slow and difficult. We crouched on the grass and panted with effort as we sliced and gouged. At last I'd cut half a V and Connie part of an O. We needed bigger tools – spades, for proper digging. We'd never finish this without being seen! I began to think we should have started last night.

In the end I gave up cutting, and improved the shape of the sooty letters instead. Connie stood back to look, while I sprinkled.

"More on the W. That's better –"

"Oi, you!" a voice bawled. "What d'you think you're doing?"

At the same moment a black dog hurtled towards us. It grabbed my skirt and growled.

It was our bad luck that an off-duty policeman was taking his dog for an early morning walk.

At the police station, Connie was in despair. "I'll be in such trouble at home!" she wailed.

"Me, too," I told her.

And what would we tell Mr Palmer and Mr Dawes? We were already late for work.

But part of me was thrilled. Might we be sent to prison? DEEDS NOT WORDS – that was the suffragette motto. Now we'd done a deed

of our own – at least, we'd *started* one. I just wished we'd had time to finish the job.

They held us at the police station until a magistrate could see us in court that afternoon. The policeman – in uniform now – described what he'd seen. The magistrate shook his head and looked at us sadly.

"You're just a pair of silly girls, copying those hoydens you've heard about," he told us.

Silly girls! That hurt.

"This time, I'll let you off with a caution," he went on. He looked down his beaky nose at us. "And you'll pay from your wages for the damage to the golf course. Don't let me see you here again, or your punishment will be a much harsher one."

A policeman walked with us to the office, to explain. Mr Palmer was disgusted with us.

"Behaving like hooligans!" he ranted. "Disgracing the name of Palmer and Dawes! I really can't have this."

I swallowed hard. I didn't want to lose my job, and I knew that Connie dreaded that too.

"It was my fault, not Connie's," I told him. "It was all my idea."

"Yes, I might have guessed that. I'm ashamed of you, Miss Frost. Leading a younger girl into trouble!"

"It wasn't –" Connie began, but he ignored her and looked us up and down.

"The state of you both! You'd better clean yourselves up."

I looked down at my dark blue skirt. We'd brushed most of the coal dust from our clothes at the police station, but there were still dirty marks.

"You must mend your ways, both of you," Mr Palmer went on. "You'll start by missing your dinner-breaks all this week, to make up the wasted time."

He gave us a heap of boring filing to sort out and we worked at it all afternoon. Now and then I tried to catch Connie's eye and smile – it was almost fun to be in trouble together – but her face was serious, her attention on her work.

CHAPTER 6

Bruised Face, Sprained Wrist

Next day Connie had a bruised cheekbone and a swollen eyelid.

"What happened?" I whispered.

"I walked into a door," she said. She didn't look at me.

"I don't believe that!" I touched the marks with a gentle hand. "Who did it?"

"My dad." Her eyes were shiny with tears, and one spilled over and ran down her bruised

cheek. "He was so angry. I'm scared when he's like that."

"Oh, Connie!" I put an arm round her. I felt awful – this was my fault. "Has he done that before? Does your mother know?"

"Yes," she sniffed. "It's how he is, after a few pints at the pub. If he's in a mood, he'll rage at anything. I try to stay out of his way, but last night he came looking for me."

I hated to think of Connie living with a man like that. My own father had been angry enough. "Are you completely stupid?" he'd shouted. "Do you want Mr Palmer to send you packing? I wouldn't blame him!"

But never for a moment would my father raise his hand to me.

We were each to lose a week's wages – ten shillings for me, nine for Connie. It meant my mother would miss the five shillings I gave her for my keep. I knew how hard she worked to

make ends meet and I couldn't help but feel bad about that.

As I cycled home later, I wondered what could be done. Elsie lived in a flat in Waltham that she shared with another girl. Maybe Connie and I could find lodgings to share? Then we could come and go as we pleased, with no one asking questions. We both earned money, even if it wasn't much.

I didn't know how to make it happen, but I had to find a way to get Connie away from her father.

At home I found a new drama. This time it was Ted who was in trouble.

My mother sat at the kitchen table with her head in her hands. Her eyes were red and her face was puffy. My father had come in from the forge and stood looking out of the window. The table was bare – no sliced loaf, no singing kettle, no sign at all of supper being prepared.

"What's wrong?" My heart leaped with fear – something dreadful must have happened.

"It's Ted," my mother said. "He's had an accident with one of the horses."

"It's the horse that's hurt, not Ted," Father told me. "He and Frank were exercising them. Slow road work, it was meant to be, with the horses not fit. But they couldn't resist racing up Spinney Hill. That grey mare Ted rides put a foot down a rabbit-hole and fell hard. She's hurt bad."

"Sea Spray!" I clapped both hands to my mouth. "*How* bad?"

"Bad enough," my father said gruffly. "They just about got her back to the stable."

"What will happen to her?" I asked, but I didn't want to hear the answer.

Father only shrugged.

I knew the fate of a hunt horse when it was no use for riding. The huntsman would shoot it. Then the kennel-man would cut its poor body into pieces, to boil up for the hounds. That was its reward.

A sense of unfairness swelled in me like a balloon.

"No!" I clenched my fists. "Not Sea Spray!"

"Poor Ted's sprained his wrist," my mother said. "In case you were wondering." She dabbed her eyes with a hankie. "I'm scared he'll lose his job, for this."

"He *ought* to lose his job!" I raged. "Frank, too – galloping about like a pair of idiots, when they weren't supposed to! If Sea Spray's lamed –" I couldn't say *shot* – "it's his fault!"

My mother shook her head. "It was bad luck. Could happen to anyone."

"Don't you act high-and-mighty, Lizzy!"
Father told me. "You're doing your best to lose
your job, too. What a pair, you and Ted – as
bad as each other. I could bang your heads
together!"

"Whatever will people think?" my mother
said, with a deep sigh.

I didn't care what people thought! I
mourned for poor, beautiful Sea Spray,
galloping so willingly for Ted, then dragging
herself home, hurt. I thought of her brown eyes
and her gentle spirit, and how she would do
anything her rider wanted.

When Ted came in, I was ready to hit him.

"Well?" Father said. "Have you still got a
job?"

As if that was all that mattered!

"What about Sea Spray?" I shouted.

"It doesn't look good." Ted's face was pale, and his left arm was in a sling, but I was too furious to feel even a shred of pity for him. "Her leg's not broken but there's serious tendon damage."

"What did Mr Colson say?" Father asked.

"He's not there," Ted said. "He's at the races."

I knew that he dreaded what Mr Colson would say when he heard.

"Well, lad," our father said. "If there *is* a war, it might turn out lucky for you. If the Army will have you."

"I know," Ted said, and he looked at the bare table. "Isn't there any tea, Lizzy? I'm parched, and starving."

"*Tea?*" I yelled. "Get it yourself!"

How could he carry on as if nothing had happened, or expect me to?

UNTIL WE WIN

I ran upstairs, and folded my pillow over my ears. If they killed Sea Spray I might hear the gunshot from here – the hunt stables were only two fields away. I couldn't bear that.

I was sick of all of them. Sick of Ted, for hurting Sea Spray. Sick of my mother, for taking his side, as if he could do nothing wrong. Sick of my father, for getting so much work from the hunt. I even hated the village, for being so backward. What would it take for things to change here, where everything carried on the same from one year to the next?

I had to leave. *Now.* I jumped up from the bed and began to stuff things into a cloth bag – hairbrush, blouse, underclothes.

I'd stay with Elsie for a night or two, if she'd have me. What next, I wasn't sure.

CHAPTER 7

A Well-Aimed Brick

"Why are men so *stupid?*" I burst out. "We'd be better off without them."

I was with Julia and Elsie in the café, at the same table as before. I thought they'd agree, and Elsie did smile and nod.

But Julia said, "It's not that simple, Lizzy. It isn't men versus women, women against men. There are men on our side, you know. Men who want fairness and equality for everyone."

"Are there?"

It had been almost all women at Hyde Park, and *all* women at our meeting. But now I remembered some men I had seen at the rally – not the police, or the man who threw the egg.

Julia nodded. "My husband Peter is my best supporter. And you've heard of Mr Pethick-Lawrence? He's been in prison. Even been on hunger strike, for Votes for Women."

I was astonished. I couldn't imagine any man I knew – Father, Ted or Frank, or the men of our village – standing up for women. They all thought Votes for Women was a big joke, if they thought about it at all.

I wanted to tell Elsie and Julia about the bruise on Connie's face, and that she was scared of her father, but just then a tall, fair woman came in.

"Ah! Here's Edwina," Julia said, and she stood up. "She's our guest speaker for tonight."

At the meeting, Miss Edwina Rutherford was first to speak. She told us that the protests were becoming too dangerous.

"Sisters – I have always admired courage and determination," she told us. "We need both, to achieve our aim. But I worry that the risks are becoming too great. Some of our comrades have been starting fires – and even using explosives. Someone will be killed before long. If people get injured or even killed, how will that help win us the vote?"

Shouting broke out. Some members agreed with Miss Rutherford, and I saw Julia nodding.

But there was dissent too. Someone called out, "We've tried peaceful protests! Years and years of letters, petitions, marches. Where's that got us? Nowhere! We need action!"

"Deeds not words!" others joined in, and soon there was so much yelling that Miss Rutherford had to shout to make herself heard.

At last the meeting broke up. Nothing was decided, and it seemed to me that the group had split into two, with each side just as determined as the other. Julia and Miss Rutherford went off together, and Elsie took me aside.

"Julia's losing her nerve," she told me. "Gone soft. But I've got a plan for Saturday. You and me. Will you help?"

I felt nervous all Saturday morning. I didn't tell Connie where I was going – it wouldn't be fair. She'd want to join us, and then her father would hit her again, and it would be my fault. She could see that I was hiding something, but I wouldn't tell her what it was.

I'd left my bicycle out of sight, behind the office building rather than in the street. In its

basket, under a folded coat, I'd hidden some broken bricks I'd taken from a builder's yard. Each one had a paper message – VOTES FOR WOMEN! – tied round it with string.

With this extra weight, it took longer than usual to ride the five miles to Waltham. The Town Hall clock chimed two as I pedalled over the bridge and looked for Elsie.

There she was, waiting, on her flat-mate's bicycle. I saw that her front basket was as full of stones as mine was.

"Ready?" she said, and I nodded. We rode on together into the market square, not speaking, and stopped outside Albright's, the big department store. In the windows we saw shop dummies in pretty dresses and summer hats.

We were both wearing jackets. Now we pulled them off to show our sashes underneath.

I reached into my basket, and Elsie did the same.

Together we yelled, "VOTES FOR WOMEN!" and hurled our bricks at the window.

The sound of smashing shocked me even though I'd caused it. Cracks jagged out from a hole in the middle of the glass. My brick, well-aimed, had crashed through and knocked the hat off one of the dummies. She rocked and teetered, pink and bald and looking somehow surprised, then toppled over.

We heard shouts near by as we threw more stones at the next window. Glass splintered and crunched. Feet came running behind us and the next moment I was grabbed from behind and wrestled off my bike. I saw that Elsie had been captured, too.

We were triumphant. This was what we wanted.

"VOTES FOR WOMEN!" we shouted, again and again, as we were bundled away.

It was the most satisfying thing I'd ever done. The weight of the brick in my hand, my voice yelling – the perfect flight of the missile before it crashed. I wished it could have lasted longer.

At the police station, I had to explain why we'd picked on the department store. I repeated what Elsie had told me. "Mr Albright sacked two shop-girls for belonging to the W.S.P.U. He had no right to do that. They hadn't done anything wrong."

We were told that the magistrate would hear our case on Monday. Till then, we were locked in the dank police cells. I wondered if anyone would tell my family where I was.

In court, we pleaded Guilty to causing criminal damage.

I knew this was a lot more serious than last time. Elsie was a previous offender, and the magistrate was the same one who'd seen me before. He gave us each a stern look before he sentenced us. I held my breath.

Two months, each. Two months in prison. I heard murmurs of approval from the public gallery, and someone said, "Hooligans, that's all they are. Lock them up. Best place for them."

Elsie threw me a joyful look as we were led away.

CHAPTER 8

Hunger Strike

Alone in my cell, I tried to feel proud rather than afraid. I gave myself strength by wondering who else had been locked up in this small bare room.

I'd already spent two long nights in the police cell, and that felt like a kind of sentence. But this was Holloway Prison, where so many brave women had been jailed. One of my heroines could have been in this same cell – Emily Wilding Davison, or Mrs Pankhurst herself, or one of her daughters. And Elsie said

that Mrs Pankhurst was in prison again *now*, after she was arrested in Hyde Park.

So I was alone, but not alone. I wasn't a *silly girl* any more. I was part of this great, unstoppable cause.

That first night, singing broke out – one weak voice at first, soon joined by others. I sang, too.

Shout, shout, up with your song!

It was 'The March of the Women', the suffragette anthem. I didn't know all the words, but now I'd learn them.

March, march – many as one,
Shoulder to shoulder and friend to friend.

I heard loud bangs, heavy and metallic.

"Stop that!" the warders shouted, as they thwacked at our doors. "Stop that singing!"

61

But we sang on, louder and more lusty than before. How could they stop us?

All the same, I had to face two powerful enemies. Boredom. And hunger.

Time dragged, marked by the chiming of a church clock near by. My cell had a high window with bars that let me see when it was dark outside.

At dusk on the second evening, I realised I'd been here for a day and a bit. *Just one day.* It felt like weeks.

But I got used to the routine. A bell woke me at 5.30 a.m. A while later, a warder lowered a hatch on my door, to make a kind of sill. She put my breakfast there – weak tea and bread, or lumpy porridge. Next I had to scrub my floor and put away my plank bed and bedding, and empty my slops. Ah yes, the slops – there was only a bucket to use as a lavatory. When I arrived I'd been made to strip naked in front

of a doctor to be weighed and measured, and to check that I wasn't hiding a knife or other weapon in my clothes. I'd hated that, but I held my head high until it was over, and pretended it didn't bother me at all – after all, the other women had gone through this, and so could I. Soon it was over and I was told to get into a lukewarm bath. My own clothes were taken away and now I wore a dress and underclothes of rough fabric.

We were led out of our cells twice a day – for chapel in the morning, and for an hour's exercise in the afternoons. Talking was forbidden, but all the same there was a buzz of secret excitement, as it was the only time we saw each other. As we walked round and round the yard, Elsie and I would try to exchange a whispered word or two.

"Julia's in here," she told me.

I looked forward to these outings, the only break in the long lonely hours. I didn't see

Julia, but it comforted me to know she was with us.

I went on hunger strike, of course. I think we all did – it was our only weapon, apart from our singing. On the first day I ate my meagre meals, but on day two I refused. Three times that day the warder put food on my door-hatch, and three times I ignored it. Soon she took the soup or bread away and slammed the hatch shut.

There was nothing to do but think about food, while my stomach growled. I thought with love of Sunday dinners at home – roast mutton or sometimes a chicken. Greens and potatoes from the garden. Hot gravy. My mother's delicious plum pie. The Irish stew she made with left-over scraps of meat. Soft sponge cakes, spread thick with jam and cream.

At first I had to bite my knuckles to stop myself from grabbing that bowl of soup. After a day or two, it got easier. My stomach stopped

wanting food, but I felt faint and dizzy, and when I went out to the exercise yard my legs trembled.

At least they wouldn't hold me down while a tube was forced down my throat. I thought of the brave women before me who'd been force-fed. Could I show such courage if need be?

I wish I could say *Yes*. But I'll never know. I knew I should be thankful that I'd never face that test.

Connie was always in my thoughts. I worried that she would worry about *me*. If only I could write and explain! I pictured her going home to her father each night. What if he got drunk again, and was angry with her? I kept seeing the marks on her lovely face, and how downcast she'd looked when she lied about walking into a door.

When I got out, I would tell her that we must always be honest with each other.

As I became weaker, I lay on my plank bed and drifted into peculiar dreams. I dreamed that I was riding to the Houses of Parliament, mounted on Sea Spray. I was wearing my sash of purple, white and green, and I was proud and strong. No one was surprised to see me, and crowds cheered as I rode past. At the Houses of Parliament I didn't stop at the door – I rode up the steps and inside, and all the men in there stared in astonishment ...

I woke up, with my neck stiff. I remembered that I was in Holloway Prison, and that poor Sea Spray must be dead by now, boiled up to be eaten by the hounds.

I cried then, for the first time in prison. Beautiful Sea Spray – she seemed as unreal now as a horse from a legend or fairy story. I cried for her, and for myself, for the freedom I had lost.

CHAPTER 9

A Different World

I knew that if I carried on refusing food, my release would come.

But freedom came sooner than I expected.

I heard the turn of a key, and my door opened. A warder flung a bundle of clothes inside. *My* clothes.

"Put these on," she ordered. "They're letting you out." And behind her sternness I saw the hint of a smile.

Let out? Was this a joke?

Weak as I was, I struggled out of the drab prison dress and into my own clothes, and soon the warder returned and flung the door open. I was led with some other girls and women – Elsie was among them! – to the gatehouse, and we signed some papers. My hand was shaking as I gripped the pen.

I still thought it was a trick, up to the moment when we stood outside and the gates were locked behind us.

For a moment I felt lost – almost as if I'd prefer to go back inside. It was so odd to be outside the prison walls. I blinked in the sunshine, not even sure where I was. I didn't recognise any of these streets and had no idea of my way home – we'd been brought here in a windowless Black Maria.

Home. Would my parents want me there, now that I'd been in prison?

Elsie and I looked at each other.

"Why –?" I began.

"Haven't you heard?" the officer at the gatehouse said. "We're at war now. With Germany."

He unlocked the gates to let a second group of women out.

"*Julia!*" I cried.

There she stood – thin from the hunger strike, her clever face lined and pale. But she held her head high, and was as smartly dressed as ever. She even wore a plumed hat.

"Ah, here you are," she said, as if this was a meeting we'd planned at the coffee shop. "You can both come and stay with me tonight. Peter's expecting us."

None of this felt real, and I wondered if I was dreaming again.

We linked arms as we headed for a bus stop near by. On the way we passed a newspaper-

seller, and saw the notice on his stand. It was a single word.

WAR!

So it was true. Julia bought a paper, and we all looked at the headlines.

BRITAIN AT WAR WITH GERMANY.

"*Now* we'll show what women can do," Julia said.

We had entered a different world. In Julia's elegant house, everything was neat and clean and comfortable. A maid took our jackets – I hadn't realised Julia was so rich – and then Julia's husband Peter came out from a back room. He kissed Julia and welcomed her home, and greeted Elsie and me as if we were proper ladies.

"There's soup ready," he said. "I knew you wouldn't be up to a bigger meal."

We sat in a smart dining room. The soup was delicious, made with real vegetables – not the sludgy stuff we'd had on that first day in prison. We sipped it, and nibbled at soft bread rolls. I'd forgotten how good food tasted. But I couldn't finish my portion.

"Sorry," I said, but Peter only smiled.

"You'll soon get your appetite back," he said. "Just eat a little at a time. I'm used to nursing Julia back to health."

He was so nice – a real gentleman, with neat hair and a short moustache. When he spoke to Julia, you could tell they were equals. I hadn't realised marriage could be like that.

Eating had tired us all out. "I'll show you to your rooms," Julia said, and she took us upstairs.

The room they gave me had its own wash stand, and a white bedspread and feather pillow on the bed, and a window that looked out to a square of grass and trees. I'd never known – or even imagined – such a lovely place.

The maid, Sally, ran a bath for me, and I lay in hot scented water, soaping myself – oh, so good, after the grimy prison bath! I sank my head under the water and washed my hair, too. After that I was so tired that I had to lie down on the bed and sleep, with my hair still wet.

I was woken by a knock on my door. "Come downstairs, sleepy head!" Elsie said, nudging me. "Lots of Julia's friends are here."

I finished combing out my hair and went down. The drawing room was full of chatter – six or seven women, all from the W.S.P.U., were drinking tea and eating cake.

As I entered, Julia said, "Here's Lizzy!"

Everyone looked at me, and some of them clapped. They were treating Julia and Elsie and me as heroines, for our hunger-striking.

I didn't feel like a heroine. I knew that others before me had been so much braver.

But soon the talk was all about War.

"I shall enrol as a nurse," one of the women said, and another, "They're going to need Land Girls, for farming."

"I've heard there'll be jobs at the War Office," Julia told us. "I know someone there."

"What will you do, Lizzy?" Elsie asked, and I shook my head. I didn't know, yet. One thing I did know was that I wouldn't be welcome back at Palmer and Dawes.

CHAPTER 10

At War!

There was a long queue outside the Town Hall. A banner was hung outside – ARMY RECRUITMENT – and it seemed that all the local men and boys couldn't join up fast enough.

"Lots of them haven't got jobs," Elsie said. "Or they don't earn much, or haven't got anywhere decent to live. They'll be paid and fed well and clothed in the Army."

There was an air of excitement – the streets were busy with people shouting encouragement to the men and boys standing

in line. A straggle of small boys played at soldiers, marching raggedly with pretend rifles over their shoulders.

I collected my bicycle from Waltham police station where it had been stored. How I'd missed it, my dear bicycle, with its chipped paintwork and shabby front basket! I had to pump up both tyres before I could ride away. When I had the chance I'd put some grease on the chain.

When I reached Denham, Mr Palmer must have seen me leave my bike by the railings outside the office. He opened the door as I walked up the steps.

"Miss Frost!" His face was red. "Come inside."

I went into his office. From behind his desk, he told me, "I don't know why you're here. There's no job for you. I did warn you. I won't

have you disgracing the company with your hooliganism."

"I know." I thought of Julia, and I stood tall. "It's a pity you think it's a *disgrace* to fight for women's right to vote. But I'm not here for work. I've brought a letter for Connie."

"Give it to me," he said.

I hesitated, then handed it over. It was only a short note, asking her to meet me later. Perhaps he'd tear it up.

Never mind. I'd return at noon.

"Thank you," I said, with a big beaming smile.

He went even redder. I think he'd expected me to plead for my job, not use him as an errand-boy.

I had two hours to spare – time to cycle home and see if my parents would speak to me. I wouldn't stay long.

UNTIL WE WIN

Our village looked exactly the same as always, but I felt different. Taller. Braver. More *myself*, somehow.

All the same, my heart was thumping as I opened the back door. To my surprise, a soldier in uniform stood inside. When he turned round, I saw that it was Ted.

My parents were both there too, staring at me. I think we were all as shocked as each other.

My father spoke first. "They let you out, then?"

"Oh, Lizzy," my mother said, close to tears. "How could you? All so that women can vote? I don't even *want* to vote – it's best left to the men. A daughter in prison! I'll never get over the shame."

"Well, you've got a son in the Army now," I said, and my voice was hard.

"Yes," Mother said, and she sounded proud. "Ted was first in the village to join up. Him and Frank."

"Because you lost your jobs?" I asked Ted.

He was shame-faced. "Yes. But not only because of the accident. The Army's taking all the hunt horses for officers to ride. All except my Sea Spray."

I looked at him, wondering what he meant.

"Sea Spray's all right, Lizzy," he said, his voice a bit softer. "She'll never be fit to ride again. But she's a mare, and Mrs Colson's favourite. They're going to breed a foal from her. She's over there in the paddock now."

"Oh, Ted!" I crossed the room to give him a hug. I could see how glad he was, how relieved.

"What about you, missy?" Mother gave me a sharp look. "Turning up as if nothing's

happened? Expecting to carry on just as you like?"

"Now, now," my father said. "This is Lizzy's home."

I looked at them all. "No," I said. "I'm not pretending nothing's happened. It has. I've been to prison. And I'd go again if I had to. But we're at war now, and there's work to do. For women as well as for men."

Ted was going back to his training camp near Denham that afternoon. And so we walked together, me pushing my bicycle.

Neither of us was going back home tonight. We wished each other luck as we parted, and I wondered when I'd see my brother again. I was staying another night at Julia's, but first I had to see Connie. I'd wait outside the office until she came out for her dinner-break.

I was early, but to my surprise she was already there, waiting.

She rushed up and hugged me as I got off my bike. "Lizzy! I've left, too. Mr Palmer told me he'd sacked you. He warned me not to get in any more trouble. I don't know what came over me. 'If Lizzy hasn't got a job here, I don't want one either' – that's what I told him, fierce as anything. And he said 'Don't be a silly girl' and 'You'll regret this'. But I won't." She was blinking back tears.

I hugged her back, tearful too. "Oh, Connie! You did that for me! But how are *you*?" I peered at her – the old bruises had faded, and there were no new ones to spoil the sweetness of her face. But if she told her father she'd given up her job ... I was afraid for her.

"Don't go home," I told her. "Or at least only for a minute, to collect your things. There's lots we can do. Now that we're at war, there are jobs waiting for us. We won't miss Palmer and Dawes a single bit."

UNTIL WE WIN

I took Connie to Julia's house, knowing Julia would help her. Peter was out at work, but Julia was there, busy writing letters at her desk.

I wish I'd told her before about Connie, and how her father hit and threatened both her and her mother. After she'd listened, and asked lots of questions, Julia wrote details in a notebook.

"I shall write to your mother, in case it happens again," she told Connie. "She shouldn't stay with a violent man, and neither must you. There are refuges run by women. Safe places to go. I'll send her some addresses – and make sure she is looked after."

It was just as important that Connie and I find work. Since yesterday, when all the ideas were flying around in Julia's drawing room, I'd decided what to do.

"I want to learn to drive," I told Julia. "Then I can work for the Red Cross, as an ambulance driver."

"Me too," Connie said. We'd talked about it on the way, and she was as keen as I was.

Julia looked at us and nodded. "You'd need to be mechanics, too. So that you could repair your ambulance if it broke down."

"Even better! I'd like that," I told her. The mood I was in, anything seemed possible.

Julia's house had a telephone, and soon she was making calls for us.

"Yes," we heard her saying in her brisk, confident way. "Two keen and capable young women. Eager to start as soon as they can."

She was scribbling on her notepad. When she'd finished, she tore off the page and handed it to us. "There you are. An interview, this afternoon. I'll give you the train fare to London."

82

So that was how I spent the war years – driving an ambulance, over in France. Taking wounded soldiers from the aid posts to the hospitals. And yes, I was my own mechanic most of the time – I changed wheels, cooled boiled-over engines, and more than once I shovelled my way out of deep mud. Hard work, long hours. I had to learn to be tough, not to give way to weeping or tiredness even when things seemed desperate.

So many died. So many. Such a cruel waste of young lives.

My brother Ted was killed in 1916, in the fighting on the Somme. He was in the first, hopeless attack on Saturday 1st July. We never learned what happened to him. We could only imagine, and hope his death was fast. I knew

by then how awful the suffering could be, from wounds or gassing.

Frank died that day, too. I hope that before he went over the top he'd found a girl happy to return his kisses.

Their bodies were never found, his or Ted's. Their names are carved in stone on our village war memorial. They're also on the Memorial to the Missing at Thiepval, but you have to look hard for them, among the thousands of others.

There were others lost from our village, too. And oh, the horses ... the horses suffered so much. I saw for myself, over in France.

It is a dreadful sin to take horses into war.

At least my lovely Sea Spray was saved. She stayed at home in her paddock and stable, and I heard that she had three fine foals.

I never married. Connie and I ... we stayed together. I never wanted anyone else.

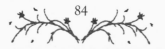

UNTIL WE WIN

Well, it's a different world now. Women got the vote, of course, but not *all* women, not till 1928. Ten years after the war ended.

1928!

What would they have thought of that, those brave women who faced prison and hunger strike, again and again? That it would take so long until we won?

And what would they say to those men and women who don't even *bother* to vote, when there's a general election?

Those suffragettes were fighting for a better world, a fairer one, for all of us. And I fought too, in my small way. I was there.

I'm proud of that.

Like *Until We Win*, *Tilly's Promise* is a beautifully written novel set at a time of momentous historical change ...

Life in this village was always the same, year after year. In fact, I'd often thought it was too much the same, and wished for a bit more change. But now ...

When war breaks out, Tilly Peacock and her sweetheart Harry are keen to do their bit – Tilly as a nurse and Harry as a soldier in France.

But the war drags on. Soon even Tilly's brother Georgie has been called up to fight, even though his mind is much younger than his body. Harry makes Tilly a promise to look after Georgie, but Harry and Tilly are about to find out that promises can be hard to keep.

Our books are tested
for children and young people by
children and young people.

Thanks to everyone who consulted on
a manuscript for their time and effort in
helping us to make our books better
for our readers.